ISBN: 978-0-692-14607-1
Library of Congress: 2018907584
Made in Grinnell, Iowa. Printed in PRC
Creator of Art, LLC Publication. www.MadeMade.com

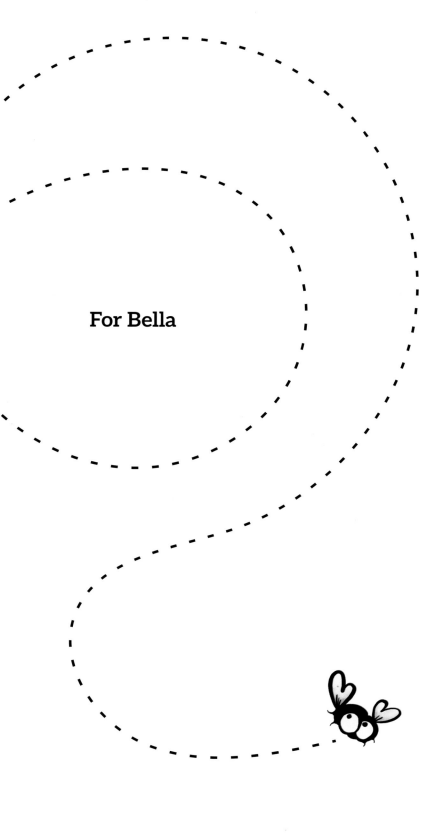

For Bella

FLIES AND CARROTS

BY RYAN MCGUIRE
ILLUSTRATED BY GAUNT

Ribbit Ribbit Rabbit,
look a fly,
Quickly!
Grab it!

With a jump and a dash,
and a **big loud splash.**

Ears flopped back, fur all **wet**

Ribbit Ribbit Rabbit do not **fret.**

The next fly that comes by,
you'll surely **get.**

Look!
From far **beyond**,
it's a fly coming across the **pond**,

and Ribbit Ribbit Rabbit is ready to eat!

With a **jump** and a **hop**,
and a **swoosh** and a **plop**,

again, Ribbit Ribbit Rabbit faces **defeat.**

Feeling down, face full of frown,
The fly lands at Ribbit Ribbit Rabbit's feet.

With a squeak and a shriek, the fly starts
to speak: "I'm not tasty to eat, I'm bitter
not sweet, but if you're hungry I know
where to find a very special treat."

With a **zoom** and a **zip**,
the fly returned from his **trip**,
something **amazing** in his **grip**,

It was a
BIG!
FRESH!
BEAUTIFUL!

CARROT!!!

Big enough
for the rabbit and fly to **share it.**

With a **munch** and a **crunch**, a **bite** and a **nibble**

their satisfied bellies began to **jiggle.**

And as the day turned to night,
Ribbit Ribbit Rabbit waves bye to the fly,
as the fly takes flight.

Ryan McGuire is a silly man who writes silly stories and does silly things. This soon-to-be bestselling author lives in Iowa with his wife and oversized cat. He's an accomplished sculptor, photographer, designer, and spontaneous dancer. You'll likely hear Ryan before seeing him because he wears 50 bells around his ankles — something he has done every day for over 14 years. Visit him at mcguiremade.com.

Blair Gauntt loves to make people laugh. Along with being an illustrator, cartoonist, and graphic designer, he is the author of "George Orwell and His Magic Penguin", a book of his "mashup" drawings that place historical and pop culture figures in situations they would never find themselves in. If Blair could have one wish it would be to grow a fully functioning prehensile tail. Visit him online at bygauntt.com.